Best Friends

Best Friends

A Special Book of True Friendship!

Poppy Bloom

Illustrated by John Blackman

SHAFTESBURY, DORSET · BOSTON, MASSACHUSETTS · MELBOURNE, VICTORIA

For my daughter Annabel,
who is also my friend.

© Element Children's Books 1999
Text © Poppy Bloom 1999
Illustrations © John Blackman 1999

First published in Great Britain in 1999 by
Element Children's Books
Shaftesbury, Dorset SP7 8BP

Published in the USA in 1999 by
Element Books, Inc.
160 North Washington Street,
Boston MA 02114

Published in Australia in 1999 by
Element Books and distributed by
Penguin Australia Limited,
487 Maroondah Highway, Ringwood,
Victoria 3134

Fran Pickering, writing as Poppy Bloom, has asserted her right under
the Copyright, Designs and Patents Act, 1998, to be identified as the
author of this work.

All rights reserved.
No part of this publication may be reproduced or transmitted or utilized
in any form or by any means, electronic, mechanical, photocopying or
otherwise, without the prior permission of the Publisher.

Cover design by Mandy Sherliker.
Cover illustration by Jan Fearnley.
Typeset by Dorchester Typesetting Group Ltd.
Printed and bound in Great Britain by Biddles Ltd,
Guildford and King's Lynn.

British Library Cataloguing in Publication data available.
Library of Congress Cataloging in Publication data available.

ISBN 1 902618 47 5

There are big ships and small ships,
But the best ships are friendships.

This book is about friends. All sorts of friends because friends come in all shapes, sizes, and skins—for animals can be our friends too.

What is a Friend?

A **friend** is someone who likes you because you are you. Even when you are grumpy or a little bit mean, a good friend will still be loyal because they know all the other good bits about you and will make allowances for your bad days.

A friend is someone who will listen to your troubles and give you a shoulder to cry on or share your joys and be happy for you.

A friend will always give you a hug if you need one.

A friend will always share their last candy bar.

A true friend will tell you the truth about yourself when you need to hear it, but that will be because they love you and care what happens to you, not because they want to hurt you.

A friend is someone you can laugh with.

A friend is always there for you.

With **a friend**, even if you haven't seen them for ages, you can immediately take up the conversation you were having when you last met.

A friend is someone you don't want to leave, no matter how much time you have spent with them.

Are You a Best Friend?

Mark your answers to these questions, then check your score at the end.

1 If your friend was invited to a party and had nothing exciting to wear, would you:

a ☐ help her jazz up an old sweater?

b ☐ lend her your best outfit?

c ☐ say: "It doesn't matter, no one will notice you anyway!"?

---

2 If your friend hadn't done his homework, would you:

a ☐ let him copy yours?

b ☐ get him to come round early before school and go through it with him?

c ☐ say: "I'll wait for you after detention"?

---

3 If your best friend wanted to go and see a band you hate, would you say:

a ☐ "Why not ask Betty Jones, she likes them"?

b ☐ "Of course I'll come!"?

c ☐ "You won't miss much, they're not as good live"?

4 If your friend was really bad at baseball and you were the team's big hitter, would you:

a ☐ tell him not to worry, sport isn't everything?

b ☐ offer to coach him in exchange for help with your spelling?

c ☐ tell him no one wants him in the team anyway?

5 If you and your friend had a row, would you:

a ☐ wait until she offered an apology and then accept it?

b ☐ phone up and say your friendship is too important to let a row spoil it?

c ☐ say "That's it!" and look for a new friend?

6 If your friend was being bullied, would you:

a ☐ tell him he can always talk to you?

b ☐ tell someone in authority and make sure he is never alone?

c ☐ tell him not to be a cry baby?

Results

Mostly a's: you're a friend but won't always put your friend first.

Mostly b's: you're best friend material!

Mostly c's: oops! Try again! Think how you'd like to be treated.

Friendship is the happy feeling you get from laughing together or sharing a secret.

If You Want to be a Best Friend ... *Do*

- ♥ remember your friend's birthday.
- ♥ compliment your friend on new clothes or a new hairstyle.
- ♥ remember friends are equal.
- ♥ keep confidences.
- ♥ help your friend revise for exams.
- ♥ look at your friend when he is telling you something important.
- ♥ call your friend as soon as you get back from holiday.
- ♥ let your friend have other friends.
- ♥ listen to your friend's point of view, however different from yours.
- ♥ share jokes.

Don't

- ♥ tell your friend she is fat.
- ♥ tell your friend he is rubbish at sports.
- ♥ watch the TV when your friend is trying to tell you something important.
- ♥ act jealous when your friend gets a new bike/CD player/soccer ball/make-up kit.
- ♥ betray a confidence.
- ♥ leave your friend out of your party invitations.
- ♥ forget your friend's birthday.
- ♥ talk about your friend behind her back.
- ♥ laugh at your friend's expense.
- ♥ not do something that you've promised you will.

Make a Friendship Bracelet

Friendship bracelets are a symbol of friendship. Anyone can wear them, young or old. Wearing matching bracelets or anklets tells the world "we are friends."

There are many ways of weaving thread to make different designs for your bracelets, and the colors you choose will be as individual as you are. Below is just one way to make a bracelet.

You'll need:

- embroidery thread cut into six 24in/61cm lengths (six strings of different colors or two in each of three different colors)
- sticky tape

1 Hold all the strings together so that the ends are level. Fold them in half and tie a knot at the doubled end, leaving a small loop of threads above the knot.

2 Secure the loop to a flat surface with the sticky tape.

3 Divide the strings into three groups of four strings.

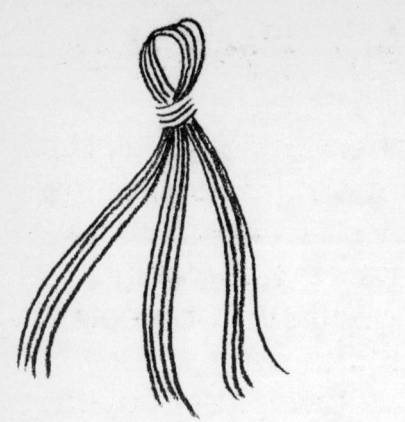 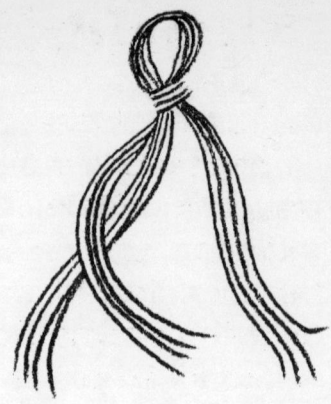

4 Take the left-hand group and cross these strings over the central group so that they are now in the middle.

5 Do the same with the right-hand strings.

6 Now do the same with the left-hand strings (which started out as the middle strings).

7 Repeat with the right-hand strings.

8 Keep doing this until you reach the end of the threads. Then tie a knot so your work doesn't come undone.

9 Take off the sticky tape.

10 To tie the bracelet to your friend's wrist, take the straight end once over the loop and then pass it through the loop and pull it tight.

Summertime Friends

"Sasha, have you got your things packed?" shouted Mrs. Malone to her daughter. There was no reply, so she marched up the stairs to her daughter's bedroom to find Sasha sitting on the end of her bed, reading a book.

"Sasha! What are you doing? We have to leave soon!" said Mrs. Malone, sitting down next to her.

"Mom, I don't want to go on my own."

"I'm sorry, honey, but you have to."

"Oh Mom, do I *have* to?"

"Look, Sasha, I know things have been difficult lately. You've had to get used to your step brother and sister, and we've all had to try and work as a family, but Ted and I think summer camp would do you good. You need to get away and have some fun."

Sasha sighed. "OK, I'll go, as long as I can come home if I don't like it."

"OK, honey, if that will make you feel better," replied Mrs. Malone in a soft tone and with a half smile.

Ted, Sasha's step-father, stood in the doorway of her bedroom.

"Everything all right girls?"

Mrs. Malone nodded.

"Well, I'll put your case in the car, Sasha!" and he picked it up and went downstairs.

Once the car was packed, they set off. During the long drive Sasha sat and stared out of the window, hardly noticing the countryside sliding past. Being an only child she had always wanted brothers and sisters, but now her mother had married again and she had one of each, she wasn't so sure it was such a good thing. Worst of all, she was secretly worried that *she* was the problem. Perhaps she just wasn't the sort of person people could get on with. Ted's two just didn't seem to like her and picked on everything she

did. They ganged up on her the whole time. She hated it all and wished life was different, that *she* was different. Now here she was being packed off out of the way.

On finally reaching the camp, they said their goodbyes and Sasha was left on her own. It was Friday evening; campers from farther away would not be arriving until the next morning. Jackie, one of the camp staff, came to greet her and showed her to her cabin. Sasha was the first in her cabin to arrive so she picked her bed and unpacked her suitcase. Then she lay on her bed, feeling sick and nervous and wondering how she would cope when the other girls arrived. Just then, through the doorway came Jackie with another girl.

"Hi, Sasha, have you settled in OK?" she asked in a perky tone.

"Yes, thanks," replied Sasha reservedly.

"This is Tanya. I'll leave you to show her where things go, then both of you come over to the main house for dinner. See ya later!" With that, Jackie left.

Sasha looked at Tanya, who sat on the edge of her bed looking at the floor. Her hands were clasped together tightly. When Sasha said, "Hi!" Tanya looked up and gave a weak grin.

"Goodness, she's more nervous than I am!" thought Sasha in surprise.

"The drawers on the left go with your bed and that room at the end is for towels and stuff," Sasha said.

"Oh thanks." Tanya gave an obvious gulp.

"Are you all right?" asked Sasha.

Tanya's eyes filled with tears. "Yes ... no ... I don't know!" she said timidly. "I'm not very good at this. I didn't want to come and I'm really afraid I won't fit in!"

Sasha stared. It hadn't occurred to her that others would feel as she did. Then it hit her. Was *that* what was wrong with Ted's children? They were younger than her. Perhaps they were afraid *they* wouldn't fit in, so ganged up together to protect each other. They had to move into her home and they must have felt more strange and awkward than she did at this summer camp.

"It's OK. I feel nervous too," she confessed to Tanya. "I didn't want to come either!"

They looked at each other and grinned.

"Hey!" said Sasha, "Let's make a pact to stick together, then maybe we won't be afraid of joining in and having fun!"

"Yes, lets. That's a great idea!"

After dinner Sasha and Tanya talked and talked until they finally fell asleep. In the morning they were woken by the breakfast bell. The few campers who had arrived the

night before were told to be back at the main house by 10 a.m. to welcome the new arrivals. Tanya and Sasha got ready and wandered over. The main hall was already filling up with new arrivals, who were put into their cabin groups. Jackie asked Sasha and Tanya to take the rest of their group back to Kingfisher cabin and show them the ropes. New faces flocked towards them, some looking just as confused as Sasha and Tanya had felt the night before.

Sasha led everyone to the cabin. There were eight new girls and she suggested everyone sit in a circle and introduce themselves, as a way of breaking the ice. Apart from one girl, Carrie, who exuded energy and enthusiasm and did cartwheels from one end of the cabin to the other, most of the girls were quite shy, and Sasha took pains to put them at their ease. Soon everyone was chatting and laughing and getting along fine. People weren't so scary after all, thought Sasha, if you took time to understand them. Most people were nervous inside.

Maybe, once this fun break at summer camp was over, she would go home and try to understand those two little horrors who might ... just possibly ... be behaving as they did because they were scared!

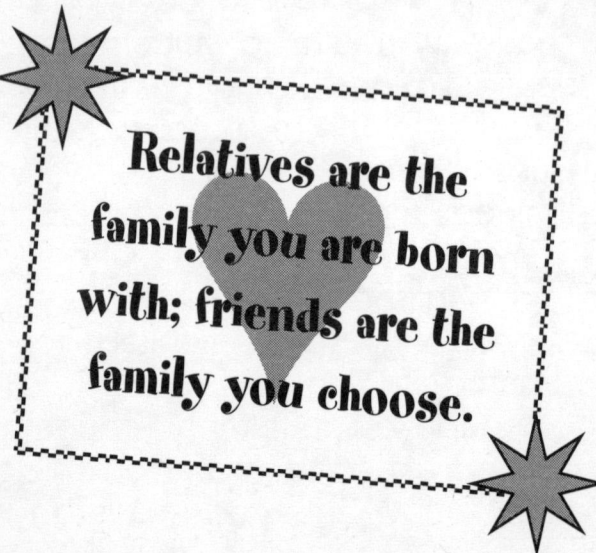

Relatives are the family you are born with; friends are the family you choose.

Friends Chill Out Together

A friend is someone you can relax with. Friendship should be comfortable. Your best friend is the one person you can be yourself with and not have to worry about what you look like. Being with your best friend is like putting on a pair of comfortable slippers—they fit you well and ease all the sore bits.

That doesn't mean you can treat your friend like an old pair of slippers and kick them about and ignore them. To have a best friend you have to *be* one. Your friend needs to feel comfortable with you too, and that will only happen if they can feel that you are not judging them, that you accept them as they are.

Who Do You Really Like?

How do you know if you really like someone? Sometimes you can be drawn to people because they look good, are great at sports, or are very outgoing, but in the end they may not be as kind or as interesting as other people who take longer to get to know. It is not always easy to see who is best friend material.

If in doubt, why not fill in the chart below. Give everyone a score from 1 to 10.

Name	Looks	Charm	Brains	Style	Loyalty	Humor	Kindness

Total up the points to decide who is really best friend material. But if you want to keep your friends, don't tell them you did this!

Scores

56-70	Hold on to this person and never let go!
31-55	Sounds like a thoroughly nice person—and no one is perfect!
21-30	Depends on where they scored the points; if it was just for looks and style, forget it!
11-20	Maybe you're lacking in judgment?
0-10	Oh dear!

Friendship Forecaster

Will you be best friends forever? What should you do at the weekend? Ask the Forecaster. Here's how to make one:

You'll need:

- a piece of colored paper 8½in/21cm square
- a black felt-tip pen

1 Fold the paper in half diagonally both ways, so that you have a big X crease on the paper.

2 Open the paper out flat again and then fold each corner in to the center of the X crease.

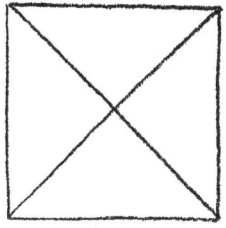 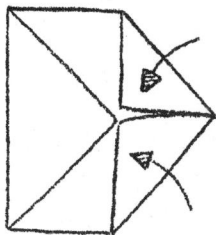

3 Under each of the four flaps write an "answer." Try and think of answers that will fit all sorts of questions. For example, "No way!," "Always," "Only time will tell."

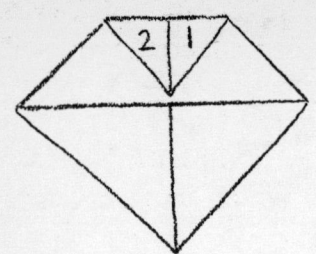 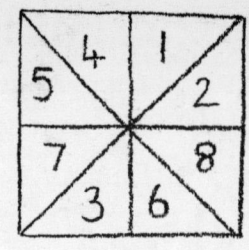

4 Fold the flaps down again and you will see that each one is divided in two by the crease. Write a number on each of the two sections on each flap. Any number from 1 to 9. Write the numbers near the center crease.

5 Now turn the whole thing over and once again fold down the four corners and write numbers on each of the small triangles.

How to use the Friendship Forecaster

1 Push all four corners together and slide the forefinger and thumb of each hand underneath.

2 Get your friend to ask the Forecaster a question and to pick one of the numbers on the outside.

3 Move your thumbs and forefingers away from each other to open the Forecaster, then move them back to close it again. Then move them out to the sides to reveal the second set of inside numbers. Go back and forth the same number of times as the number your friend picked.

4 When you stop, ask your friend to pick one of the inside numbers and then repeat step 3.

5 Finally, ask your friend to pick one more inside number and lift the flap to see the answer.

Net Buddies

Ellis Brown and Carlotta Mendes became good friends without ever seeing each other. They are not alone. Many people who use the Internet have found friends on it, but here is just one story.

Ellis had just got her new computer and was going to use it for a school project. She had to find a pen pal in another country. The school had lists of people who wanted to be pen pals but Ellis decided to log onto the Internet and leave a message on a forum, saying she wanted a pen pal, and see who wrote back.

Every day for a week Ellis came in from school and checked her e-mail. One day there was a message from a girl in Spain.

Her name was Carlotta and her mother was Spanish and her father English. She had lived in London until she was two, when the family moved to Spain. Carlotta's father had a souvenir shop for tourists near the beach and they lived in a house not far out of the main town. Carlotta was twelve and liked swimming and lots of outdoor sports.

As Ellis read more of the letter she found lots of things they had in common. Ellis wrote back to Carlotta and soon, after much correspondence, they became good friends.

Carlotta invited Ellis and her parents to Spain for the summer. As both of the mothers spoke on the phone once a month and got on well, it was decided they would go.

Two months went by and holiday time came around. After a long car ride, a plane flight, and another car journey, they reached the Mendes' family home—a square, white building alongside many others on the side of a hill. Ellis shared Carlotta's room and her parents took the spare room. The house was small yet light and spacious looking. They settled in for the night, and in the morning breakfast was served on the verandah.

The day was gorgeous and Ellis couldn't wait to explore. Carlotta had a surprise for her. They were to take part in a street festival.

After breakfast the parents all went sightseeing and dropped Ellis and Carlotta off at the hall where the costumes were being made. Ellis's face lit up when she saw all the huge, brightly-colored costumes and puppets. They joined in with the other children, gathering paper and materials in shades of red, and started to plan their masks and cloaks. For the next three days they went to the hall to finish their costumes, decorating them with beads and paper streamers. The theme of the group they were in was fire, so lots of bright oranges, reds, and yellows filled the hall.

Friday came and the costumes were put on. Everyone got ready for the march through town. Carlotta's and Ellis's parents went to find a good place to watch along the route. Then the procession started. There were stilt-walkers, fire-eaters, jugglers, clowns, dancers, and bands. Large paper puppets were held aloft on long poles. In amongst all this the children of the town danced along in groups, each

depicting one of the four elements: earth, air, fire, and water.

Ellis found the whole event utterly thrilling. She had never done anything like that before. She had such fun with Carlotta and had found so much more than just a pen pal.

Making Friends on the Internet

Until you really get to know someone you contact via the Internet, it is not advisable to give them your home address and telephone number. Also, make sure that a grown-up knows what you are doing.

Friendship is for Real

You cannot pretend friendship. You have to really like each other for this to happen.

Friendship takes time. Best friends are not made overnight. To be easy enough with someone to become their best friend you have to know them very well. That comes with doing things together, listening, talking, and sharing both fun and sad times.

Best friends are equal. You can't have a close friendship if one person acts as if they are smarter or prettier than the other person. Best friends know that they may each be good at different things, but that doesn't make one of them better than the other one. Best friends value and respect each other. Best friends like the different bits of cleverness in each other.

Friendship Flip

A good drink to cool off with on a summer's day

Mix together:
- ½ pint/300ml milk
- 1 small carton low-fat yogurt
- 2 teaspoons sugar

Then add one of the following:
- ½ cup peach juice
- 1 banana, mashed
- 3 drops rose water

Mix all the ingredients in a blender, or put then in a thermos bottle or jug with a tight-fitting lid and give then a *very* good shake.

Pour the mixture into two glasses, add straws, and enjoy!

Friends Give Flowers

Friends the world over give each other flowers. From as far back as ancient China, people have used flowers as a code to express their feelings, or to send a message. These meanings are not so commonly known now, but they remain in some of the expressions we still use: "rosemary for remembrance," or "a four-leaved clover for good luck."

Here are some flowers and their meanings:

Blue periwinkle	The start of a friendship
Buttercup	You are childish
Cornflower	You are delicate
Dahlia	You have good taste
Fern	I am sincere

Garden daisy	I agree with you
Gardenia	I love you in secret
Honeysuckle	You are sweet
Iris	I have a message for you
Lavender	I will be true
Orange blossom	Your purity equals your loveliness
Pink rose	Be my friend
Red rose	I love you
Sweet William	You are perfect
Tulip	You will be famous
Zinnia	I think of you

The Postman's Cat

Jim lived on the edge of town, in a tiny cottage in the middle of a row of tiny cottages at right angles to the main street. By day he was the postman, delivering the mail on foot within the town and to the grand houses by the river, or cycling farther afield to the outlying farms and villages.

One of his rounds took him past a dingy second-hand shop whose window was full of chipped crockery, ancient bric-à-brac and piles of old clothes. Sometimes he would glance in as he strode past whistling, but mostly he barely gave the shop a second

look. One day, however, a movement in the window caught his eye. The pile of rags in the far corner was moving.

He took a closer look. No, it wasn't rags! A thin tabby cat, with bones sticking out so painfully it tore at his heart, was gingerly rearranging herself, trying to find some comfortable spot on the tattered coat she was lying on. He stared. How could anyone let a cat get into such a state? She could only be fed just enough food to keep her alive. He walked on, muttering to himself about people who shouldn't be allowed to have pets.

All during his round his mind was on the cat, and when he had finished he walked back the way he had come. Reaching the shop, he went inside.

"Yes," said the surly woman behind the counter, in the sort of voice that hinted he had better not have come in actually wanting to buy something!

"'Er," he said, "It's about the cat!"

"The cat?" The woman sounded puzzled.

"The cat in the window. Do you want it?"

"Oh, that lazy animal. Good for nothing. We got it to catch the mice but it's too lazy to bother! Anyway, it's not for sale; we're going to have it put down!"

"But if it's no use to you! I'd pay well," he pleaded.

"I told you, it's not for sale!" repeated the woman. Just then a large man appeared in the doorway that led through to the back of the shop.

"You heard her," he said. "Clear off!"

Friends are always on your side

Jim went, but not without stopping to stroke the cat as he went towards the door.

The next day was his day off. It was warm and sunny and, not having a garden, Jim sat just inside his open front door, watching the world go by and reading a book. He had just reached the end of a chapter when a tiny movement caught his eye.

In through the door came a cat. A very thin cat. The cat from the second-hand shop!

"Hey," said the postman. "How did you find me?"

The cat stood and looked him squarely in

the eye as if she were seeing into his soul and taking his measure. Then, satisfied, she walked past him and explored the room. From the front room she went into the kitchen, then up the stairs to the bedroom and bathroom. It was a small house and her tour of inspection did not take long. Finally she curled herself into a small ball on the hearthrug and slept.

Jim rushed out to the shops and bought some fresh fish, cans of cat food, and a small, catnip mouse. He left the door open in case she wished to leave (in the days of this story it was still safe to go out and leave your doors open). When he came back she was still there. She never left. She made her choice and for twenty-five years she and the postman lived as happily as any two friends who truly love each other.

After Jim and the cat had shared the house for several years, war broke out. Although he was too old to go to war, Jim joined the Home Guard and made himself useful in ways that took as much courage and energy as the Army demanded of a younger man.

The town he lived in was not an important one so it was not a target for bombing like many of the larger towns and cities were. Children from these cities were sent for safety to live in the country and smaller towns. They were called "evacuees." One day, when Jim was on the other side of town, helping two children settle into their new home with Mr. and Mrs. Murchison, a soft scratching and a loud "meow" were heard at the door of their house. Someone opened the door and called out: "There's a little tabby cat here!"

Jim straightened up from the bunk beds he was repairing and went with everyone else to look at this strange cat that was making such a noise outside. It was his own little friend. As soon as she saw him she began to meow. She walked away a few steps, then turned and looked at him. She continued to do this—meow, walk a few steps, turn. When no one moved, she ran and pulled at Jim's trouser leg, then began to walk away again.

"She wants me to follow her! I don't know why," he said, "but she is my friend and it must be something very important to make her come across town and find me like this."

"How did she find me?" he marveled. "Maybe we should all follow her. I have a feeling that's what she wants."

They all trooped outside—Jim, Mr. and Mrs. Murchison, and the two bemused children from London, who were already thinking that life in a country town was very strange and wishing they could go back to the familiar bustle and noise of the city.

The cat kept just ahead of them, stopping every few paces to make sure they were following. They had walked a good long way and were beginning to think they were all very foolish and the cat was leading them on a wild goose chase, when she stopped suddenly and sat down, then turned to look back at the house, now a speck in the distance. They all turned—and just at that moment, from a clear blue sky, an enemy plane roared into sight, streaked across the countryside and dropped a bomb right on the Murchison's house. It was completely flattened. Only a pile of rubble remained.

For what seemed hours but was only moments, they were all rooted to the spot with shock and horror. Then the world sprang back into life. Sirens sounded as fire engines and the ambulance rushed to the scene. People came running to offer help and comfort. An empty house was found for the Murchisons to live in; folk gave them furniture and bedding, clothes and food, and gradually order was restored and life went back to normal. But for Jim the postman nothing was ever the same again, for he never forgot how his little tabby friend had loved him so much that somehow she had found her way across town to a place she had never been before to find him and save his life.

A friend will always try your cooking—and say it tastes good.

Friends Trust Each Other

Best friends trust each other. Trust takes time. First you tell someone a little thing about yourself and see if they can be trusted with that. Then they tell you something, and soon you are swapping secrets and telling each other your worries. Best friends can be trusted to keep secrets. Best friends can be trusted with knowing the real you.

Best friends are loyal and trustworthy. Friends trust each other with precious possessions. You wouldn't lend everyone your favorite CD or book or sweater, but you'd trust your best friend with it. You'd trust them because time has shown you that they will take care of it because it is important to you.

Friendship Photo Frame

Why not make a special frame for your friend's photograph, or to put a photograph of yourself in as a present for your friend.

You'll need:
- cardboard
- colored paper
- glue
- scissors
- ruler
- pencil
- paints or felt-tip pens

1 Cut a piece of colored paper at least ½in/1.5cm larger than the photograph. Glue the photograph in the center of it.

2 Place the paper on some thick card and draw round it with a pencil.

3 Remove the paper and draw another rectangle around the one marked on the card. Make it at least 1in/2.5cm wide. Cut around the outer edge of this second frame, so you have one large rectangle with a frame shape marked on it.

4 Repeat steps 2 and 3 on another piece of card. This time, cut around the inner and outer edges of the outer frame to give you just a card frame.

5 Place a dab of glue at the four corners of the colored paper and stick this carefully in the center of the card.

6 Draw or paint a design on the frame shape. Leave this to dry and then glue it carefully in place over the backing card.

7 Instead of a painted design, you could glue pasta shapes, beads, shells or buttons onto your frame.

Horse of Dreams

Donna lay in bed staring at the small square of sky she could see from her window. She sighed. She was fed up. Having to stay in bed most of her life was no fun. She wished she could go out into that beckoning blue and play with the children whose laughter floated up to her. But she couldn't. Even sitting in the special chair they had got for her tired her out. How she hated her silly, floppy body and muscles that didn't work. She began to cry.

"Oh, love!" said her mother, coming in the door at that moment. "Oh, if only there was something I could do. I'd give anything for you not to be like this!" and her eyes too filled with tears.

Donna felt mean. She knew her mother felt guilty that she had been born with this disease. But it wasn't her fault. It wasn't anyone's fault. But it was hard to bear.

And now her father had gone. That made Donna feel guilty in her turn. If she had not been born like this maybe he would have stayed. Donna knew how hard it was for her mother to juggle a job with looking after her. That was why she tried not to moan when she spent long hours on her own. Her mother did her best, but she couldn't work miracles. What a mess it all was.

Her mother had brought lunch up on a tray and they ate together in companionable silence. Donna reached out and gave her mother's hand a squeeze. "It's OK!" she said.

"No, it's not," she replied. "It's far from OK."

There was silence for a while.

"As soon as I can get the money together," said her mother, "We'll go to New York and see that doctor who specializes in your condition. Then it will be OK. He can do wonders, they say. He'll sort you out!"

Donna sighed again. Her mother had been saying this for ages. They had a scrapbook full of newspaper cuttings and articles about a surgeon who had devised a way of helping people like her. But it took a lot of money to pay for the operation and the waiting list was long. Donna didn't hold out much hope but she pretended she did because she knew it was what drove her mother to work so hard. The hope of helping Donna kept her going.

A friend will always give you a hug.

Donna wished she had a friend to talk to; that would help. Someone to giggle with and share secrets. Someone to watch TV or listen to tapes with. But no one came because no one really knew her.

Dusk fell and Donna snuggled down into the pillows, still staring at the patch of sky that was gradually turning dark blue. A small white speck appeared in the sky. A cloud? Snow? It grew bigger ... and bigger. Whatever was it? It looked like ... no, it couldn't be ... yet, it did look like ... a horse with wings!

Donna stared. The horse grew larger as it came nearer, its strong wings beating smoothly against the night sky. It came right up to the window. Without so much as the flutter of a wing feather it came right through the window and landed beside the bed.

"Hello Donna!" it said.

Donna gulped. She pinched herself. She seemed to be awake. "Who are you?" she asked.

"I am the Horse of Dreams," it replied, white and beautiful beside her bed. "I have come to make your dreams come true!"

"Oh," said Donna. She couldn't think of anything else to say.

"Climb on my back," said the horse, "and we'll be off!"

Donna, who found it hard to make her legs and arms do anything without help, threw back the bedclothes and climbed onto the soft, white back.

"Put your arms around my neck," said the horse, "I will not let you fall."

Donna held tight. The horse spread his wings, sprang lightly into the air and they were away, through the window and climbing into the night. The wind blew past Donna's cheeks and ruffled her hair. She leant more closely against the horse's neck and felt his warm body take the chill from her own. She could feel the ripple and pull of his muscles under his skin as his wings beat up and down, up and down, like the pulse of some strange tide carrying her away from all she knew.

On and on they went, until Donna dozed against the horse's neck while he flew through the night and across the world.

"Here we are!" said a soft voice in her ear and a velvety nose nuzzled her neck. Donna woke with a start. They had landed in a field whose grass was greener than any field she had ever seen. Not that she had seen many, except on TV, but she knew this green was what green should be. Playing in the field, running, skipping, laughing, walking, and talking were children of all ages.

"Off you go!" said the horse. "This is where you belong! Here you can do all you dream of!" and he nudged her gently .

Donna slid from the horse's back and took a step forward. Her legs worked! She took another step—then, before she was ready, a crowd of laughing girls came by, grabbed her hand and dragged her off to join their game.

Sometime later, Donna did not know how much later, the horse came for her. Sadly she climbed back up, not wanting to go home to the world of bed and wobbly legs.

"Cheer up!" said the horse. "There's always tomorrow!"

"You mean I can come back?" asked Donna.

"Of course!" smiled the horse. "Say goodbye to your new friends and we'll be off!"

Friends! She had friends now! Donna was so happy she thought she would burst!

"My goodness!" said her mother the next morning. "You look well! There are roses in your cheeks! If I didn't know better I'd say you'd been outside!" and she laughed at her own silliness. Donna laughed too.

Every night, as dusk turned to darkness, the horse came for her. In the dark-blue

47

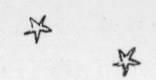

light he carried her to the Land of Dreams and in the hour before dawn he brought her safely home. She learnt the games the children played in the street below, and many others besides. Her legs grew stronger with all the exercise they had at night and riding the horse strengthened her arms and back. Her loneliness eased because she had many friends to share her secret world, and so the days were helped along by thoughts of the night. All this went on and no one knew.

One night she said to the horse, "Will my special dream ever come true? Will I ever be able to walk in my world and make friends with the children who live nearby?"

"It is already coming true," said the horse. "for you are becoming truly who you are and when that happens, all dreams are yours."

Now she was stronger, Donna could sit for a while on the edge of her bed, looking out of the window at the children below. Once one of them looked up and she took courage and waved. He waved back. The children began to make a point of looking up and waving at her. Then one day her mother came in to say some children were downstairs, wanting to see her.

In they trooped, three girls and two boys, looking even more shy than she was. The old Donna would have slid down under the bedclothes, paralyzed with awkwardness, but the new Donna had practice now in getting to know people and making friends, so she chatted away to them until they were all laughing and cracking jokes together. The children asked if they could come back again, and would she like them to take her out in her wheelchair. She said yes to both.

One night the horse told her this was the last time he would take her to the Land of Dreams.

"You no longer need me," he said. "Your dreams have almost come true. Dreams don't come true overnight, but little by little as we make them happen. Soon, what you did in the Land of Dreams, you will be doing in your world. You do much of it now: you have friends to talk and laugh with, you go out with them and join in their games. Soon you will walk and run with them into a bright future where you can make many more of your dreams come true."

Donna was sad, but not so sad, for she had her friends now and a new, exciting life ahead of her.

"There are others that need me," said the horse. "Other children need to visit the Land of Dreams and learn what wonderful things they can do if they reach out and try."

Friendship is helping each other with homework.

Friendship in the Stars

Find out which star sign your friend was born under, then look it up in the list below to see if the description matches.

Aries (21 March–20 April)

Ariens like casual clothes, yet can look stylish. Although they may spend a lot of money on clothes, they often have one favorite item of clothing which they wear and wear. Always in a hurry, they can charge into people in their rush to get somewhere. Your Arien friends may like horse riding, going off for long walks or on adventure holidays, because they will have lots of energy that they need to use up in exercise. Whatever they do, they have lots of enthusiasm, like to win, and go for what they want.

Flower: Honeysuckle **Color:** Scarlet
Gemstone: Diamond
Possible Future Career: Professional sports person, artist, engineer

Taurus (21 April–21 May)

Taureans often have hair that flops over their face. They aren't wildly fashionable and tend to like floral patterns. They love comfort, and rich food—lots of it, so your Taurean friend could be the one being sick after the party! They don't like to be hurried and can be slow to learn, but once they have learnt something, they never forget it. Taureans have strong feelings about things and like to take their time over making decisions. They are patient and kind but when they become angry, which isn't very often, stand clear of the explosion! They can be stubborn.

Flower: Pink rose **Color:** Pale pink or pale blue **Gemstone:** Moss agate

Possible Future Career: Actor or actress, beautician, architect

Gemini (22 May–21 June)

Geminis are very fashionable and like to wear the latest fads, possibly making some of their own clothes. Does your Gemini friend have bright ideas for altering sweaters, cutting the sleeves off last year's shirts, sewing bows and bits of fur on things? Geminis are often tall and slender, with fine hair cut short over bright, alert eyes. They love jewelry, bags, belts, and hats, and often spend all their money on these. Geminis know a little about a lot of things, and will tell you what they think about most things—and probably wave their arms about while doing so. They find it hard to stand still and don't like to do the same thing for long. Just as you are getting interested in something, your Gemini friend will probably want to be moving on to a new hobby or activity. Geminis enjoy being with people and are good at communicating.

Flower: Lavender **Color:** Yellow
Gemstone: Agate
Possible Future Career: Sales assistant, teacher, receptionist

Cancer (22 June–22 July)

Cancerians often have long, untidy hair and small eyes, and a tendency to sit or stand slouched over with rounded shoulders. They like soft shades, but can dress quite sloppily, often spoiling a nice dress by wearing ancient sneakers with it, or teaming shabby sweat pants with a new sweater. Your Cancer friends will probably have a closet full of useless things because they hate to throw anything away, or they may collect badges or bugs or model cars—anything. Cancer people are kind and helpful; they value their friends and like to hang on to them.

Flower: Lily **Color:** Gray **Gemstone:** Pearl
Possible Future Career: Teacher, cook, artist

Leo (23 July–23 August)

Leos have a mass of thick hair and hold their heads high. They love clothes—designer clothes, colorful clothes, rich fabrics, and anything that is dramatic. Your Leo friends may well want to decorate their bedrooms in fairly startling colors. They are not good at hiding their feelings, and, more than any other sign, they tend to express how they feel in their body language, so you will probably be in no doubt when they are happy or in a bad mood. They are good organizers and born leaders, and just love a party, so can be great fun to be with as long as they don't get too bossy! Leos hate to lose their friends and will be more upset than most if a friendship breaks up.

Flower: Sunflower **Color:** Orange
Gemstone: Ruby
Possible Future Career: Designer, soldier, actor or actress

Virgo (24 August–22 September)

Virgos tend to wear dark colors; and they like to keep clean and tidy so usually have a neat, sleek look. They often have quite a pointed nose and chin, and their walk can be quick and sharp. Your Virgo friends may have a habit of clasping their hands when not talking or doing something—have a look next time you are together. As they are usually talkative you may need to tell your Virgo friend to shut up now and then!

Although they talk a lot, they don't miss much of what goes on around them, and may well notice details about something that other people miss. Virgos like to be helpful so are good friends to have!

Flower: Cornflower **Color:** Dark blue
Gemstone: Opal
Possible Future Career: Policeman, doctor or nurse, teacher

Libra (23 September–23 October)

Librans are naturally attractive with good figures. They love romance and wear romantic clothes. They can often see both sides of an argument or a problem and like to keep the peace, so this often makes it hard for them to make up their minds and reach a decision. They can appear lazy, but if you think about it, your Libran friend will usually get a job done by working hard and fast, thus leaving more time for play. Librans like company. They are kind and understanding and your Libran friend will be sympathetic to your problems and worries, and probably good at calming you down. They may well be good at music or singing.

Flower: White rose **Color:** All shades of blue
Gemstone: Sapphire
Possible Future Career: Lawyer, alternative therapist, counselor

Scorpio (24 October–22 November)

Scorpios like the feel as well as the look of clothes, so they may choose to wear leather, velvet, silk, and satin. They often have large foreheads and deep-set eyes, and are rarely tall. Scorpios know exactly what they want to do and go for it, plunging right in to new projects, homework, friendships, whatever. They can be stubborn and downright uncooperative—in fact, a real pain in the butt! Like a scorpion with its sting in the tail! However, they also value their friends and will do a lot to make a friendship work. So if your Scorpio friend is being annoying, just remember that he or she really wants to be with you.

Flower: Geranium **Color:** Dark red
Gemstone: Amber

Possible Future Career: Miner, banker, racing driver

Sagittarius (23 November–21 December)

Sagittarians are interested in so many things they don't bother much about clothes, so can look quite scruffy. Their favorite colors are often purple and royal blue. They need lots to do and think about, so are often to be found reading rather than playing sports. Sagittarians usually like people, smile easily, are full of enthusiasm, and get everyone joining in whatever is going on. Your Sagittarian friend may enjoy dancing or basketball, archery or garage sales, but whatever it is, they'll do it with all their energy and get you involved as well.

Flower: Dandelion **Color:** Purple
Gemstone: Topaz
Possible Future Career: Publisher, explorer, veterinarian

Capricorn (22 December-20 January)

Capricorns are often tall with bony wrists and knees and lots of thick, heavy hair, a wide face, and eyes that look at you steadily. They can be very stylish, but don't dress to draw attention to themselves. They aren't very daring but now and again will have a silly spell, surprising their friends who thought them a bit dull. Your Capricorn friend may be a person who likes to do things in a certain way and finds it hard to change. Capricorns often need to stick to a routine and can be quite obstinate about this, complaining loudly if they have to change something.

Flower: Pansy **Color:** Dark green
Gemstone: Amethyst
Possible Future Career: Builder, dentist, office worker

Aquarius (21 January–18 February)

Aquarians often like to wear blues and turquoise, colors which balance their pale eyes. They can be good, kind, helpful friends, but they are also very private people, so it will be hard to get to know an Aquarian. They can get very absorbed in what they are doing and forget time passing, which may include forgetting they were supposed to be doing something with you! They can also be stubborn, and once their minds are made up they don't easily change. Your Aquarian friend may have an unusual hobby or interest, because Aquarians are often very bright and have unusual minds. They make excellent inventors.

Flower: Orchid **Color:** Turquoise
Gemstone: Aquamarine
Possible Future Career: Scientist, artist, social worker

Pisces (19 February–20 March)

If you have a Piscean friend, look at their feet! Pisceans often stand with their legs crossed, making the shape of a fish's tail! These are the folk who like ethnic clothes and often have wild, unruly hair. They are kind and caring, but like to be left alone in their own space to dream their dreams. Pisceans like to go their own way; they don't like rules and regulations and find it hard to stick to them. Like fish swimming in the sea, your Piscean friend may often change his or her mind at the last minute. Don't get mad—just be glad you have one of life's dreamers for a friend, for these are the people who often give us beautiful paintings or poems.

Flower: Moss **Color:** Silver
Gemstone: Moonstone
Possible Future Career: Artist, dancer, poet

Friendship Cookies

Make these with your friend on a rainy day.

You'll need:

- 3oz/85g margarine
- 2oz/55g caster sugar
- 2oz/55g light brown sugar

- 6oz/170g self-raising flour
- 1 egg
- 4oz/110g chocolate chips

You'll also need a mixing bowl, cup, fork, wooden spoon, flat knife, weighing scales, wire cake rack, two flat baking trays.

Before you start, turn the oven on to 180°C, 350°F or gas mark 4. Never, ever use a hot stove without permission or without a grown-up nearby. Make sure you wear oven gloves to handle hot trays and always place them on a heat-proof surface. Never bend down in front of the oven and then open the door; the rush of hot air will burn your face. Open the door first, then bend down.

1 Put the sugars and the margarine into the mixing bowl and squash them all together with the back of the wooden spoon. Keep squashing and stirring as fast as you can until the margarine is paler and fluffier and the sugars are well mixed into it.

2 Break the egg into a cup. To do this, hold the egg in one hand and bang it sharply against the side of the cup. A crack will appear. Hold the egg over the cup and pull your hands slightly apart and upwards so that the egg falls into the cup. Make sure no bits of shell have fallen in, then beat the egg with the fork to mix the yolk and the white.

3 Pour some of the egg into the margarine and sugar and beat it with the wooden spoon until it is well mixed in. Keep doing this until you have used up all the egg.

4 Tip the flour into the mixture and beat again until you have a thick, smooth paste. Then do the same with the chocolate chips.

5 Drop lumps of cookie mix about the size of a walnut onto the baking trays. Space them out well and flatten them slightly with the back of the spoon.

6 Bake the cookies for ten minutes until they are just turning brown. Take the trays from the oven and put them on a heat-proof surface.

7 Leave the cookies for about one minute, then slide a flat knife under each one and pop it onto a cake rack to cool and harden.

When the cookies have cooled you can both enjoy eating them—or put them in a tin and save them for your lunch boxes.

The Secret Friend

Danny is a business man, in charge of a large advertising agency. There is not much Danny is afraid of, yet he remembers to this day how lonely and scared he was as a small boy growing up in the Irish countryside, far from any other children to play with. The worst day was when he had to start school. This meant a long and lonely journey on a country bus, to go and spend all day with children he had never met. Here is his story.

Danny felt sick! Tomorrow was his first day at school and he didn't want to go! Every time he thought about that new, strange place his tummy felt funny and he wanted to cry. He lay in his bed, silent tears rolling down his cheeks as he looked around the small, familiar room and wished he could stay in it for ever.

The next day Danny woke up with the sick feeling still in his tummy. He got up and put on his new trousers and sweater. They felt stiff and strange and unfriendly and didn't help the sick feeling.

Downstairs he couldn't eat his breakfast but his mother made a fuss and said he couldn't go to school on an empty stomach. She changed her mind when he began to cry and said not to worry, she'd packed him a good lunch to take with him and he could fill up on that.

Ten minutes later he stood waiting by the gate for the school bus, with his small hand tightly held by his mother's. His new school bag was on his back and inside it were his new pencil case and the new lunch box. Everything was new.

When the bus came his mother bent down and gave him a quick kiss. "Off with you now. You'll enjoy it, you'll see!"

She sounded brisk but her eyes were damp. Since his father had died she had to manage the farm alone, and although she would dearly have loved to take Danny to school that day and every day, she just could not leave the farm.

Danny climbed aboard the bus and once the driver had made sure he was safely sitting down, they clanked and rattled on their way. Danny thought his heart would burst with grief and terror and that he would die before he got to the dreaded school, or—worse—be sick.

Just then a small voice said: "Hello!"

He jumped in surprise. Beside him on the seat sat a small girl.

"My name is Angela," she said.

Danny stared at her. Then it all got too much for him.

"I wish I didn't have to go to school," he

said aloud. "I want to stay with my mother," and tears rolled down his cheeks.

"Oh, school's fun," said Angela, "you'll enjoy it."

"No I won't," said Danny. "I don't want to go! I'm frightened. I won't know what to do and I don't know anyone. I want to stay at home."

"Everyone has to go to school," said Angela "and it can be scary at first, but you'll soon make friends with the other children and then it will be fun." "Anyway," she added, "you will know someone. You know me and I'll be going!"

"You?" asked Danny in astonishment.

"Yes!" said Angela. "I'm going with you!"

From that moment Angela went with Danny everywhere. At school he kept quiet about her as he knew by instinct that no one else could see her, but at home she had her own chair at the table, her own pillow next to his, and often ate the same things as Danny.

Danny's mother accepted Angela as if she had always been part of the family. When Danny had a sandwich she made Angela one. She remembered to hold the door open for her when they got in the car, and she always kissed Angela good night when she tucked Danny up in bed.

Angela stayed with Danny for over a year. Then, one day, as he and some of his school friends were playing around the farmyard and barns, he suddenly realized he had not seen her for a week or more. Try as he could to find her, he never saw her again. Oddly enough, his mother stopped talking to her about the same time. He could only imagine she went to find another lonely child who needed a friend.

Ten Good Stories About Friends

The Friends
Rosa Guy

The Adventures of Huckleberry Finn
Mark Twain

Best Friends
Francine Pascal

Anne of Green Gables
Lucy Maud Montgomery

The Butterfly Lion
Michael Morpurgo

Animal Friends
Dick King-Smith

The Secret Garden
Frances Hodgson Burnett

The Wind in the Willows
Kenneth Grahame

Charlotte's Web
E. B. White

The BFG
Roald Dahl

The Children of Holbeck House

The Swanson family were off to the country. They had inherited an old house from Great Aunt Josephine—a distant aunt, you could say, as the children had never met her. Yet it was the children—Jane, aged twelve, and her eight-year-old brother Sam—who had been left the house.

"Come on guys, take your stuff into the cottage and pick your rooms!" shouted Clare, Jane and Sam's mother. The children raced each other upstairs. Their father, David, brought the rest of the luggage in. The family had managed to get a holiday cottage only a few miles from the village where the house was. Over supper they discussed their different ideas of what the house would be like.

"I bet it's a big scary place like the Addams family would live in," said Sam, squashing his carrot with his fork.

"Don't be silly! It will be a beautiful mansion where balls were held," said Jane, imagining a grand staircase down which she was descending in a ball gown.

"Well, I think we all have to be prepared

for the fact that it is probably falling down," butted in their father.

"Oh David! Don't be so miserable!" laughed Clare. "It's probably a perfectly ordinary house!"

"It's probably as cracked as Aunt Jo herself!" David muttered with his mouth full.

"You shouldn't say things like that!" Clare said, looking at the children and laughing with them.

After breakfast the next day they piled into the car and set off, with David driving and Clare reading the instructions the solicitor had sent them. Once through the village they turned off the main road into a winding lane. About a mile along on the left they came to large iron gates set between high stone walls. Huge metal letters across the gates spelt out: HOLBECK. Jane and her mother hopped out of the car to pull open the gates, which looked heavy but moved easily, so someone must have oiled them recently. They drove slowly up the drive through the beautiful enclosed garden to a circular area in front of the house. David switched off the engine and they all got out of the car. The house was square with pointed turrets, and in the middle was a studded wooden door with a huge lion's-face knocker.

"Wow!" said Sam, looking up at it.

"Come on, let's go in!" demanded Jane in excitement.

"I'll go in first," said David, getting out the key the solicitor had given him.

"Now, children, don't run off!" cautioned Clare. "Stay close to your father. We don't know what state this place is in!"

Slowly they pushed the door open and edged inside the house. They were standing in a square hallway with a large staircase in front of them on the left-hand wall. To their left was a door, to their right another door, and in front of them, to the right of the stairs, the hallway led to a wide wooden door. It was difficult to see much as there was no light at all.

Jane looked round. On either side of the front door were tall, shuttered windows. "Hey, let's open these!" she said, rushing over to one and flinging open the shutters. Her mother opened the others and the place came to life. The light revealed a beautiful mosaic-tiled floor and a polished wooden staircase with a banister rail held up by carved wooden lions.

Jane was off. She rushed into the room on the left and again threw open the shutters. The others trailed after her.

"Wow!" exclaimed Sam again.

"It's huge, and in immaculate condition," remarked Clare.

"Isn't it gorgeous!" breathed Jane.

It was a living room, Victorian in style, with everything of the best quality. Off that room was a study, lined with oak paneling. A large oak desk stood in front of the fireplace and heavy, red velvet curtains framed a long window that looked onto the rear garden.

On the other side of the hall they found a dining room with a table large enough to seat twenty people, and off that a magnificent library, some of whose shelves contained many old-fashioned children's books.

Through the door at the end of the hall was a massive kitchen. Stone slabs covered the floor. A large, well-cared for black range sat in pride of place against the chimney breast. Brass pans and utensils were hung around the room and in the center stood a long wooden table. You could almost smell the aroma of cakes baking and stews bubbling.

"Come on! Let's go see upstairs!" shouted Sam, dashing off, with Jane close behind.

"Be careful!" David shouted after them.

Upstairs there were four bedrooms and a surprisingly modern bathroom. The master bedroom was in red, with a four poster bed;

Friendship means you have to be a friend back.

the green room had an ordinary double bed; and the other two rooms—one decorated in blue and one in yellow—were large enough to each have three single beds and still have plenty of space for chairs and tables. At the end of the landing Jane and Sam found another door. It was locked.

Jane dashed off to fetch her father, who came back with a selection of keys. One fitted and the door opened onto a steep, narrow staircase upon which shafts of dusty sunlight fell. They climbed up.

At the top they found themselves in a large attic room. Old toys were strewn everywhere—a rocking horse, a large dolls' house, a jack-in-the-box.

"Oh my goodness, look at all this!" Jane said, flabbergasted.

"Your mother and I are going outside to explore the gardens. Do you want to come or stay here?" asked David.

"We'll stay!" they both chorused, not taking their eyes from the mass of stuff in the room.

The children began to walk among the toys, looking and touching. It was odd that everything in the house was like new, yet at the same time old, especially considering the house had not been lived in for many years, as Great Aunt Josephine had spent the last years of her life in a nursing home.

Looking among the treasures, Jane found some paintings of different children and then a box of pictures and poems, obviously done by children. Against one wall was a long mirror set in a wide, gold-leaf frame. Jane looked at herself in the mirror, then froze. She felt breath on her cheek, and as she stared at her reflection a small, white face appeared beside her own, then the complete figure of a girl in a blue dress with a white pinafore took shape. Jane leapt back, letting out a half-yelp, half-gasp.

"Sam!" she yelled.

"What's up ... oh, my goodness!" said Sam, coming to stand behind his sister. As they watched the child walked out of the mirror to stand before them. "Hello!" she said.

"Are you a ghost?" asked Sam, hiding slightly behind Jane.

"That I am!" said the girl. "My name is Laura. Welcome to my home!"

"Your home?" asked Jane.

"Yes! Do you like our house?"

"It's brilliant, but what do you mean our house? Are there others here?" Jane asked.

"No! There's just me here, but the house is mine and Jo's!" replied Laura.

Do you mean Great Aunt Jo?" exclaimed Jane.

"Yes, my sister Jo!"

"Gosh! I didn't know Great Aunt Jo had a sister! I suppose you are Great Aunt Laura then!" said Sam, laughing.

"What happened to you, if you're still little?" asked Jane, almost at the same time.

"This house is special; it's alive. It loves children. Jo and I always used to have our cousins and friends here. This house was always full of fun; a magical place to be. Jo and I have a nick-name for it—we call it 'Never Never House.' You know, like Peter Pan!"

At this point Jane and Sam were sitting cross-legged on the floor, listening in amazement.

"One morning," went on Laura, "we were playing on the landing, Jo and I, and Tom,

Libby, and William. I was messing about, balancing on the banister, pretending I was in a circus. I overbalanced and fell—and here I am and have been for over seventy years."

"Oh, that's awful!" exclaimed Jane.

"So why did Aunt Jo leave us the house?" enquired Sam.

"Jo's son, Adam, wanted the place. He wanted to tear it down and build lots of houses on the land. He didn't care what Jo wanted, so she left it to you two so I would be protected, because she knew you would be able to see me and I would still have a home. She knew too that you would enjoy the memories of the children of Holbeck House."

"Don't worry, Laura," said Jane, "we'll look after the house, and you."

The three of them talked for ages. Jane and Sam had inherited so much more than just a house. They now had a new friend as well as the tales of the lives of Laura and Great Aunt Jo.

Jane and Sam's parents loved the house so much they moved into it, and fun and laughter returned to Holbeck. They lived there happily, all five of them, creating a new chapter in the history of Holbeck House.

Friendship Puzzle

Hidden in the grid are 21 words relating to friendship. Can you find them?

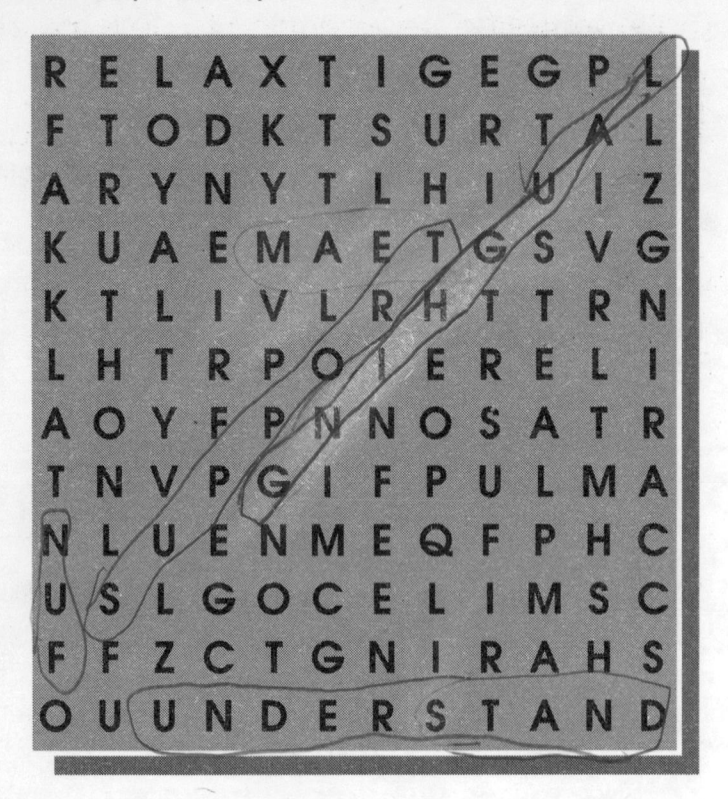

```
R E L A X T I G E G P L
F T O D K T S U R T A L
A R Y N Y T L H I U I Z
K U A E M A E T G S V G
K T L I V L R H T T R N
L H T R P O I E R E L I
A O Y F P N N O S A T R
T N V P G I F P U L M A
N L U E N M E Q F P H C
U S L G O C E L I M S C
F F Z C T G N I R A H S
O U U N D E R S T A N D
```

Answer on page 80.

Friendship is Giving

Friends like to give each other presents. Sometimes the best gifts are those you make yourself. One nice thing to do is make your friend a birthday or friendship card.

1 Trace around the outline of this drawing, or draw your own scene, then transfer it onto a folded piece of colored card.

2 Now color the picture in.

3 Write your own greeting inside.

Friendship Puzzle answer

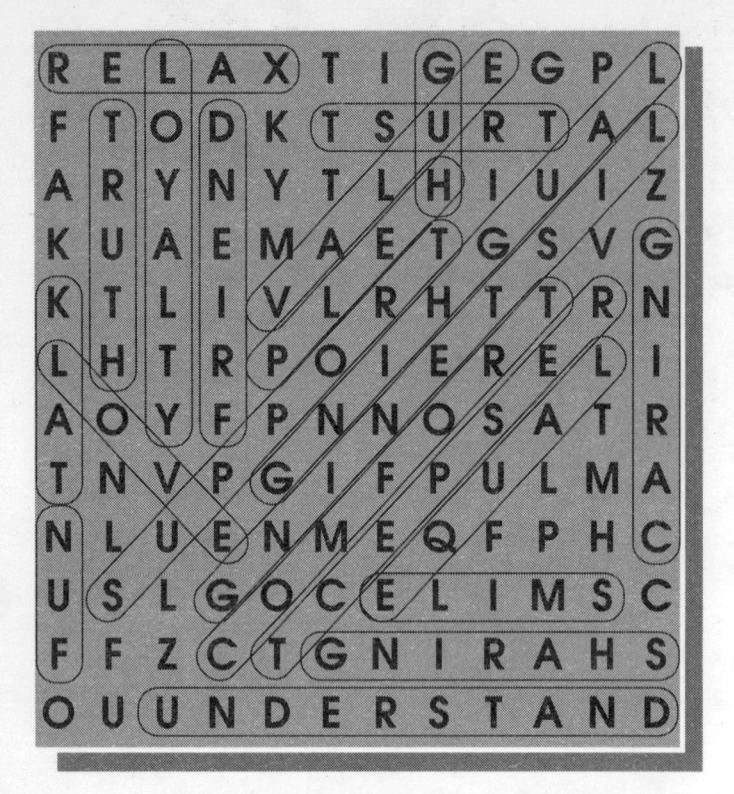

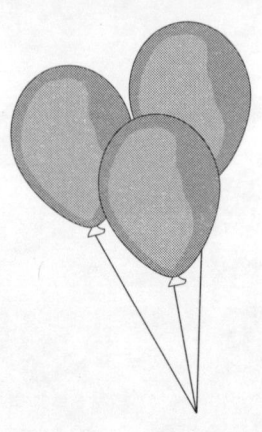

R	E	L	A	X	T	I	G	E	G	P	L
F	T	O	D	K	T	S	U	R	T	A	L
A	R	Y	N	Y	T	L	H	I	U	I	Z
K	U	A	E	M	A	E	T	G	S	V	G
K	T	L	I	V	L	R	H	T	T	R	N
L	H	T	R	P	O	I	E	R	E	L	I
A	O	Y	F	P	N	N	O	S	A	T	R
T	N	V	P	G	I	F	P	U	L	M	A
N	L	U	E	N	M	E	Q	F	P	H	C
U	S	L	G	O	C	E	L	I	M	S	C
F	F	Z	C	T	G	N	I	R	A	H	S
O	U	U	N	D	E	R	S	T	A	N	D

Make a Special Envelope for that Special Card or Gift

You will need:

- a piece of paper 14in x 12in/35cm x 32cm (use fancy wrapping paper or draw your own design on plain paper)
- ruler and pencil
- glue or double-sided sticky tape

1 Draw parallel lines on the paper, as shown.

2 Cut away the shaded areas.

3 Fold along the dotted lines, as shown.

4 Glue or tape flaps in position.

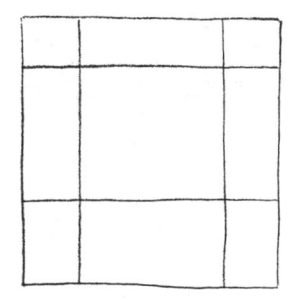

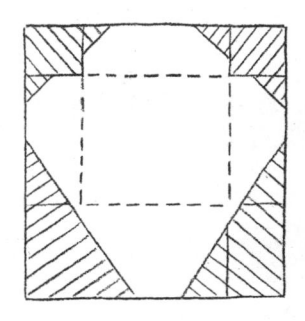

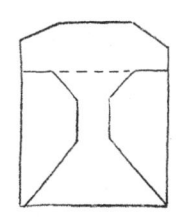

Japanese Friendship Dolls

Sidney Gulick, an American, had been in Japan in the 1920s. He thought that if children in different countries could become friends they would be less likely to want to fight each other in wars when they grew up. He felt that children should learn that outside differences of dress and language do not mean inside differences in hearts and minds. He wrote: "Living in different lands ... we need to learn that we appear as strange to other people as they do to us; our language sounds as queer in their ears as their languages do in ours. But in spite of all differences in appearance, we are all related ..."

One of his ideas was the "Doll Plan." He arranged for the children of America and the children of Japan to exchange Friendship Dolls.

Each year, on the third day of the third month, Japanese families celebrate the "Festival of Dolls," when they display dolls that have been handed down for generations. Sidney organized a huge campaign to have blue-eyed American dolls sent to the school children of Japan. A total of 12,739 dolls were sent, each with its own steamship ticket and passport. In return, over 2,610,000

Japanese children each gave one *sen* so that a hundred Tokyo craftsmen could make fifty-eight dolls to send to America.

When the dolls arrived in Washington they were greeted with a special welcoming ceremony, and then, from January to July, 1928, the dolls traveled round the country so that people could see them. Finally, each state was given one doll, with some of the larger states getting more than one. Many of these dolls are still in museums and Heritage Centers.

The Japanese Friendship Dolls were beautiful. They were 32in/81cm tall, and dressed in silk kimonos embroidered in gold. They wore silk "tabi" socks and carried parasols; many of them came with their own furniture, tea sets, screens, and writing materials, all of the finest craftsmanship.

Around 5.3 million people participated in Dr. Sidney Gulick's gesture of friendship and goodwill, and today his grandson continues to help Japanese and American children exchange Friendship Dolls.

When Friendships End

Friendships end for lots of reasons. If only one person wants the friendship to end, then it is hard on the other person. People change as they grow older. Sometimes they change too much to be your friend any longer.

These are some of the reasons why friendships end:

- You move on to different schools.
- One of you goes to college, the other out to work.
- The things you each like to do change as you get older.
- One of you moves to another town.
- Your friend talks too much behind your back.
- One of you gets a boyfriend or girlfriend.
- You have a huge row.

Friendship is chilling out together.

What to do when a friendship ends:

- Know that it is OK to feel really sad.
- Try to remember all the good things about your friend, not just the way in which he or she has changed.
- Understand that if your friend doesn't like you any more that doesn't make you an unlikeable person. Plenty of other people will think you are wonderful!
- Know that it is OK to feel mad if your friend has let you down badly.
- Feel mad or sad for a while, then put that feeling away and let it go.
- Remember that if your friend said something nasty about you, that is only an *opinion*. It may not be the *truth*.
- Get to know as many new people as you can. A new friend will be out there somewhere.

The Sea Child

Hi! I'm Laine, and before I start my story I'll introduce you to my parents. My mother, Maggie, is an interior designer, so she's into color analysis, feng shui, and that kind of stuff. I guess she's pretty cool. She's tall, with short blonde hair, and knows what not to say in front of my friends!

My father, Adam, isn't so blessed in the "don't embarrass-your-daughter" department. He's a doctor. You'd think this would come in useful sometimes, but no, *au contraire*! You can't get away with pretending you are a little bit more ill than you really are—know what I mean? And, typical of fathers, he tries to be more with it than he is, and it really shows. But he means well.

This is my story, as I wrote it in my diary.

Monday, July 5

The thing that really sucks at the moment is my life. We are moving. I like my home town; it's not too big but it's not small enough to be really boring. I like my school and don't want to leave all my friends. My father is moving to a new practice in a tiny harbor town over on the east coast. Mom says it's not too far for me to see my friends at weekends, but it just won't be the same.

Wednesday, August 11

Well ... we've moved into our new house. It seems OK. I have a really big room which looks out onto the sea, but I'd rather be looking out of my old window and seeing my friends riding their bikes up and down our street.

Thursday, August 19

As I thought, there isn't a lot to do round here. Anyway, I decided to go exploring on my bike today. I had been riding around for ages and hadn't found anything interesting when I found myself down at the old fishing harbor. I rode out onto one of the small wooden jetties by the rocks, got off my bike and sat on the side of the jetty, splashing my feet in the water.

I was feeling as though I would never be really happy here. If we hadn't moved, I'd be playing out with my friends instead of moping about on my own. I collected a handful of stones from the rocks and began to throw them one by one into the sea. The afternoon was drawing to an end and I knew I should be going home soon, but I wanted to sit and mope a bit longer. I wasn't in the mood for anything else. I threw another stone.

Suddenly there was an almighty splash, and I was showered with water. My stone wasn't that big, surely?

"No, it wasn't!" said a girly, giggly voice. Looking up in great surprise I saw on a rock this little girl with a tail like a fish.

"Who are you?" I asked, curiosity forcing my question.

"My name is Sylvie, and you seem pretty sorry for yourself at the moment!"

I looked at her, still a bit stunned at her appearance.

"Are you all right ... er ... I'm sorry, I don't know your name."

"I'm Laine. Are you a mermaid?" I asked hesitantly.

"Yes, that would be a human interpretation, but in my world we are sea children," Sylvie replied.

"Have you been down there all the time?" I asked, pointing to the deep, salty water.

"Most of it ... but you need cheering up. There's no fun in feeling down, so I just don't!"

"What do you have in mind?" I asked, still not quite sure if I was talking to something from my imagination.

Sylvie gave a huge smile. "Meet me here same time tomorrow and you can meet some of my friends. They'll cheer you up!"

"But what are we going to do?" I yelled, as Sylvie slid back into the sea. Realizing she had gone, I got on my bike and rode home, wondering if I was cracking up. Was I so lonely that I was imagining things?

Friday, August 20

I got up, still wondering if I had imagined yesterday's event. The only way to find out was to go to the harbor in the afternoon and see if Sylvie was there. I arrived much earlier than I had the day before and sat for ages and ages on the jetty, not throwing stones this time, but staring around me into the deep, green sea, hoping to see a smiling face staring back at me. But there was nothing.

I was just about to give up and go home when up popped Sylvie.

"Hi, Laine! I'd like you to meet two of my friends, Darwin and Coral!"

Behind Sylvie were two dolphins. I just stared. They fixed their gentle gaze on me and smiled. I felt the smile go right inside me, curling round the sad bits and the things I'd left behind and joining them up to today and hope. Their smile was like sunshine.

In no time at all I was in the water, being pushed and pulled through the waves by Darwin and Coral. It was so much fun. They chattered and clicked to each other and to me, and in a way I understood them. Sylvie was right. They did cheer me up.

Saturday, August 28

My parents and I are going for a picnic so I won't be able to go to the old harbor today. Still, there's always tomorrow. My friends will wait for me. Sylvie was right when she said her friends would cheer me up. Now she and Darwin and Coral are my friends. The best friends I've ever had. Harbor-town life isn't so bad after all; in fact, it's really great fun.

Friendships are life's flowers.

Party Time

Parties are fun. It's even more fun to throw a party with your friend. You could make it a joint birthday party, a Halloween party, end of term party, or just a party because you feel like a party! Getting it ready together can be just as much fun as the party itself. Here are some ideas to get the party going.

Color Party

- Ask everyone to come dressed in a particular color, say red or blue.
- Hang up decorations and balloons in that color.

- Ice some home-made muffins or small cakes in your chosen color.

- Make sandwiches with colored fillings. In a bowl, make a fairly mushy filling—with egg, cheese, cream cheese, or tuna, for example—then add a few drops of vegetable dye and keep stirring and mashing until it is all mixed in. Then spread on slices of bread and cut into sandwiches.

- Decorate the party room with rainbows painted on large sheets of white paper, or make a rainbow mobile to hang up.

Animal Party

- Make some animal masks from card. To do this, just draw the shape of the animal's head on a thin piece of card, make two holes for the eyes, and then tie a piece of ribbon or string to each side of the mask so it can be tied at the back of the head.
- As guests arrive, give everybody an animal mask. From then on they have to "talk" using the sound that animal makes. This can be hilarious.
- Cut out your sandwiches in animal shapes.

Flower Party

This is a nice idea for a summer party.

- Set up a table in the backyard and have ready some face paints. As guests arrive, paint small flowers on their cheeks or turn their face into one large flower.
- Pin the name of a flower on each guest's back. They then have to find out, by asking the other guests, which flower they are. The only rule is that those asked a question can only answer "yes" or "no."
- Cut your sandwiches in the shape of a flower.
- Get some small, clean, plastic flowerpots

and fill them with party goodies for each guest. You could include flower stickers, tiny plastic bugs, jelly worms, a packet of flower seeds.
- If you live with an adult who is a good gardener, see if they can spare a tiny plant or seedling for each guest to take home in a pot. If would be even more fun if guests could pot their own plant to take home.

Masquerade Party

This is great fun if you like dressing up. You'll need to prepare for this by getting in some extra-wide crepe paper in bright colors, or some old sheets that you can cut up. You'll also need some white or colored card, scissors, paste brushes, lots of glue, sequins, beads, glitter dust, feathers, scraps of beautiful material, buttons, and anything else you can think of for decorating costumes—plus long scarves, dressing-gown cords, belts, lace, string, etc. for tying round waists.
- Make invitations in the shape of a masquerade mask and write them out giving details of when and where the party will be. For example, "You are invited to a Masquerade Party on Saturday, April 6, at Jane's house, 206

Rockwood Drive. Time: 6 p.m. Please bring your dancing shoes."

- Before the party, make T-shaped, floor-length dresses from crepe paper or sheeting. To do this, cut a rectangle of material twice as long as the measurement from your shoulder to the floor. Fold it in half and cut a shallow semi-circle out of the center of the folded edge (to put your head through). Make enough dresses for everyone—in suitable sizes! If you are making them out of crepe paper in different colors, make two extra dresses so that your friends have a choice.
- Before your guests arrive, cover the floor of one room with newspaper.
- When everyone has arrived, get them to choose a dress.
- Now comes the fun part! Using the glue and all the bits and pieces you have provided, everyone has to decorate their ball gown.
- When the gowns are finished, your guests can put them on and tie them round the middle with the scarves or cords.
- Then, put on some music and dance until it is time to go home!

Who Said What?

Below are some famous quotations about friends and friendship and the names of the people who said them. Can you fit a name to each quotation? (If you don't know, have fun guessing!)

Mel B, John Lennon and Paul McCartney, Matt Leblanc, Virginia Woolf, Taylor Hanson

1 "I have lost friends, some by death ... others through sheer inability to cross the street."

2 "I get by with a little help from my friends."

3 "Us five do argue occasionally. It's only natural when we're together all the time, but it's never anything serious."

4 "I've really grown to care about these people. And I think we all feel the same way."

5 "It's great to be best friends with your brothers. Then you've got friends for life."

Answers

1 Virginia Woolf, 2 John Lennon and Paul McCartney, 3 Mel B, 4 Matt Leblanc, 5 Taylor Hanson

Friends Share Secrets

ELLOHAY RIENDFAY

What better way to keep a secret than to have your own special code that no one else knows. Histiaeus, a Greek ambassador to Persia, sent secret messages back to Greece on the head of a slave. The slave's head was first shaved, then the message branded on his skull. After his hair had regrown, he was sent to Greece. When he arrived, his head was reshaved to reveal the message. I'm not suggesting you do anything as drastic as this, but you could invent a code—either written or spoken—that only you and your friend know.

Here are some ideas to get you going.

Spoken Codes

For these, you use ordinary words, but slip other sounds into them. For example:

1 If a word begins with a *vowel*, add WAY to the end of it.

2 If a word begins with a *consonant*, move the consonant to the end of the word and add AY after it. If the consonant sound is made up of two letters, move them both to the end.

Here is a sentence using this code:

RIENDSFAY AREWAY IFE'SLAY LOWERSFAY ALONGWAY HETAY AYWAY
(Friends are life's flowers along the way)

Another idea is to add a sound, such as "OP" or "DIB" in front of each vowel, or after each consonant in a word. Here is a sentence using "OP" after each consonant.

FOPROPIENOPDOPSOP MOPAKOPE TOPHOPE WOPOROPLOPDOP A HOPAPOPPOPIEROP POPLOPACOPE
(Friends make the world a happier place)

If you can learn to say your code really fast, you can baffle everyone.

Written Codes

A written coded message usually needs to have letters or numbers put in the place of the real letters in the words. You need to agree beforehand what your secret alphabet will be. A simple one is to give each letter a number:

A	B	C	D	E	F	G	H	I	J	K	L	M
1	2	3	4	5	6	7	8	9	10	11	12	13

N	O	P	Q	R	S	T	U	V	W	X	Y	Z
14	15	16	17	18	19	20	21	22	23	24	25	26

Here is a sentence in this code:

1 19.20.18.1.14.7.5.18 9.19 1 6.18.9.5.14.4
23.1.9.20.9.14.7 20.15 8.1.16.16.5.14

(*A stranger is a friend waiting to happen*)

Greyfriars Bobby

In the city of Edinburgh, Scotland, is a graveyard called Greyfriars. Once, a long time ago, the graveyard had been a garden belonging to the Grey Friars, monks of the order of St. Francis, the saint who loved animals. During the long years of its history, some of them bloody, many of them cheerless, the garden lost its orchards, gained a wall, and finally became a resting place for the dead. Visitors to Edinburgh today go to see the famous castle, to visit the nearby churches, and to look at the statue of a small dog and marvel at the love and loyalty shown by this tiny Skye terrier.

When Bobby was a puppy he went to live with John Gray and his family in one of the small houses crowded into the narrow lanes of the city. John was a policeman and he was allowed to have a dog to work with him. He chose Bobby, a lively little dog who, in spite of his size, was brave and fearless in helping his master to break-up fights and catch criminals.

Policemen worked a long day in the last century, and because they were not allowed to go into a café or inn for food, they carried bread and cheese or meat, and a flask of tea or soup, to have on their one break in the day. John Gray always shared his meal with Bobby.

Number 6 Greyfriars Place was a pie shop at that time and although they could not go into the restaurant itself, once their day's duty was done John and Bobby would sometimes go to Number 5 where the piemaker lived and sit by the fire eating pies.

Bobby loved John Gray and John Gray loved him. Out together in all weathers, often soaked to the skin, cold, tired and hungry, they relied on each other for company and support. They were probably each other's best friend.

The winter of 1857 was cold and wet and John and Bobby were often soaked and shivering as they went about their work. John Gray began to cough. In the end his cough was so bad and his chest hurt so much, he could not work. He lay on his bed at home, Bobby beside him. Early in 1858 he died.

On the day of his funeral the family walked behind the coffin to Greyfriars burial ground. With them walked Bobby. The coffin was lowered into the grave and covered with earth. The family turned to go home, but Bobby stayed put. One of John Gray's children picked Bobby up and carried him, struggling wildly, back home.

Bobby refused to eat. He sat in a corner, threw his head back and howled. He whimpered and cried and scratched at the door. In desperation, someone let him out. He never came back.

Bobby made his way back to the graveyard, crept through the iron railings and found his master's grave. For the next fourteen years, until his own death, Bobby stayed with his friend. In bad weather he sheltered under a nearby table-gravestone, lying on some sacking put down for him by the Greyfriars' gardener. In really bad weather James Anderson, a furniture maker who lived nearby, took him into his home, but Bobby only stayed long enough to escape the worst of the storm or snow, then he went back to be with his friend.

Local people passing by would give him pieces of food. Sometimes he would go to the pie shop, as he and John used to do, and be fed a hot pie. When the pie shop changed hands, the new owners took on the task of feeding Bobby, as did the people who followed them.

In 1867 a new law was passed which said that anyone who owned a dog had to have a license for it. Any dog without a license could be destroyed. Licenses were expensive and Bobby had no one to buy him one. Or did he? The Lord Provost of Edinburgh had heard about Bobby. He knew of the dog's faithfulness and loyalty to a friend long dead and thought to himself that few humans loved and grieved as much as that little dog did. He decided that Bobby should be saved and that because the Town Council owned the Greyfriars burial ground they should pay for Bobby's license. As he was head of the Town

Council, he paid the money due and had a fine collar made for Bobby. On it was a brass tag inscribed: "Greyfriars Bobby, from the Lord Provost, 1867, licensed."

As the years went by Bobby became frail and ill. On a Sunday morning, January 14, 1872, Bobby died and went to join his master at last. Mr. Traill, the new owner of the pie shop, and a few friends secretly buried Bobby in the Greyfriars graveyard, as near John Gray's grave as they dared. His grave is not marked, but that does not matter for his legend and his memory are as alive today as he once was. He will continue to be remembered as a small creature who for friendship's sake braved years of cold and hunger and loneliness to be near the person he loved.

Famous American Friends

Susan Anthony and Elizabeth Stanton

Susan Anthony was born in Massachusetts in 1820, into a Quaker family. When she was seventeen she became a teacher, and soon began to do something about the injustices she found. Later, when she was thirty, she met Elizabeth Stanton, and they became life-long friends. Like Susan, Elizabeth had the same burning desire to make things better for people, especially women and slaves. Throughout the rest of their lives the two women worked together, setting up organizations, and touring the country lecturing. They tried to get people to understand how wrong it was to keep people in slavery, and to convince them that women should be allowed to vote and to divorce their husbands if they were unhappy. At the time, all of this was quite shocking for men to hear. They were very brave women because they stood up and said things that upset those in power.

Orville and Wilbur Wright

Orville Wright was born in Dayton, Ohio, in 1871, four years after his brother Wilbur. As the boys grew up they became friends as well as brothers. As small boys they were both interested in mechanics and as they grew older they both became gripped with the excitement of making man fly. They studied hard and experimented a lot until they knew all there was to know about the science of flying. Because of their close friendship they worked well together; after they had solved one of the world's biggest puzzles and built a heavier-than-air machine to lift a human into the air, they took it in turns to act as pilot or cameraman to record for history how they did it. If they had not been such good friends, prepared to work hard and solve problems together, we may never have heard of them.

Jane Addams and Ellen Gates Starr

In 1889 these two women founded Hull House in Chicago. This was the first step in their huge, life-time project to bring security, justice, employment, and education to the many women and children who were excluded from most of the things we take for granted today. Through the efforts of Jane and Ellen and the many other women who lived in Hull House, hundreds of men and women found work and were provided with day care for their children. In addition, they had access to an art gallery, libraries, a theater, and a museum, and were able to take classes in music and art. The women of Hull House worked to protect immigrants, stop child labor, and to ensure that children were educated. They also set up the first Juvenile Court in the United States.

All these friends achieved more together than they would have done on their own. Because their friendships were strong and because they believed in the same things and had the same dreams, they worked together to make those dreams come true.

Make a Cartoon of Yourselves

Many cartoons feature characters that are friends: Wallace and Gromit, Mickey and Donald, Rugrats. Why not create your own little characters, one for you, one for your friend. You could draw them on badges to wear, or really go to town and set them in their own cartoon strip.

Looks

Cartoon characters are funny or appealing because normal things about them are exaggerated. Noses are big, mouths are huge or very small, or have lips that stick right out. The character may have hair that is short and spiky, or fuzzy like a mad professor, or it may have a long fringe that flops everywhere, or sticking-out plaits. Take some of the *characteristics* of yourself and your friend and exaggerate them to make a funny cartoon character.

Personalities

Make them as like you and your friend as possible. Exaggerate your personalities. If one of you is tidy, make that character really over-tidy. If one is often late, make the character always dreadfully late, rushing about like a mad thing, scattering belongings everywhere in their haste to get somewhere. If one of you collects things, turn the character into a fiendish collector of something really odd.

Trying to work out the cartoon characters will help you get to know your friend better—and you'll have lots of laughs along the way.

Friends Never Forget

Mike and Ben had been friends for as long as they could remember. Their parents lived next door to each other and they had grown up together. They were almost exactly the same age. Ben was born on a Monday and Mike was born on the following Friday. Often they shared a birthday party.

Of the two, Mike was the quieter child. He was shy, good at art and music and not very good in a fight. Ben was big and breezy. He was good at all sports, laughed a lot, and was always ready with his fists to defend himself, Mike, or anyone else.

It was a friendship that shouldn't have worked, but it did. Mike taught Ben to slow down, look, and listen to the world around him. He loved all creatures and hated to harm anything. Stray cats and dogs, bugs and birds, all found a safe haven with Mike. Underneath his bluster and bravado, Ben secretly admired Mike. In his turn, he helped Mike hold his own in the school playground, coached him in tackles and passes, and generally lightened up his friend's more serious nature.

Once, when they were quite young and

just getting used to their first bikes, they had ridden off for the day along the lanes and out into the country. A few miles from home, on a quiet lane normally free of traffic, a car shot round the corner in the middle of the road and clipped the edge of Mike's front wheel. Somehow Mike managed to stay on, but he lost control and he and the bike wobbled dangerously across the road and tipped into the ditch.

Ben rushed to the rescue. The car was long gone. Mike and the bike lay in a crumpled heap in the ditch. Mike was bleeding from cuts to his head, face, arms, and legs; and one arm was broken. The bike's front wheel and handlebars were buckled beyond repair.

"Don't cry!" said Ben. "There's plenty of room on my bike! We'll soon get home!" He tore a strip off his shirt and bound up the worst of Mike's cuts. As he did so he cheered his friend up with some corny jokes. Then he helped Mike onto the saddle, straddled the bike himself and they swayed and wobbled home.

The years passed and the two boys went away to separate colleges and into different jobs, but they still kept in touch. When war broke out and all young men were called up to be soldiers, Mike and Ben found themselves in the same regiment. For all of them, war was a terrible thing—not just the noise and the mud and the terror and the senselessness of it, but the horror of having to kill other people. Even Ben found it worse than his worst nightmares, but, as a born fighter, he took pleasure in the skills he developed and the loyalty and friendship of his fellow soldiers. For someone like Mike, who was happiest playing his violin, reading poetry, or walking in the pleasant green fields of his homeland, to lie in trenches filled with mud and blood, waiting to kill or be killed while the noise of battle raged all around, the whole thing was almost unbearable.

Soon, neither of them had time to think

about what effect this was having on them for they were caught up in of one of the fiercest battles of the war. They fought until they were exhausted and still they fought on, until only a few men were left standing and the dead and dying lay in piles on the ground. Among them lay Ben, too wounded to move himself to safety. The remaining members of his regiment had retreated, and were too far away to help him. A few enemy soldiers were walking among the bodies, rescuing any of their own men who were still alive, and finishing off the others. They drew nearer to Ben, who closed his eyes and waited to die.

Suddenly he heard the sound of galloping hooves and cries from the enemy soldiers as they fell to the ground. He opened his eyes to see Mike looking down at him. He was on horseback.

"Don't cry," said Mike. "There's plenty of room on my horse! We'll soon get home!"

He got down and gently lifted Ben up onto his saddle, climbed up behind him and, clasping his friend to his chest with one arm, took them both to safety.

Sleepovers

Sleepovers with friends are fun, although sleep is usually not something you get much of. Talking, eating, giggling, and listening to music—maybe, but sleep? Forget it!

Why not arrange a sleepover for your friends. Here are some ideas for a fantastic night.

Make some invitations

Cut some colored card or paper into rectangles about 4in x 3in/10cm x 7.5cm. Put a few fancy stickers in the corners or run a glue stick around the edge and then drop some glitter dust onto that. Finally, write the invitation in the middle.

Dear Jennifer
Please come to my
sleepover
on Friday at 8 p.m.
from Sarah

Make a sleepover record book

Buy an exercise book or scrapbook and cover it with pretty paper, or use plain paper and decorate it with your own design. Inside, paste photographs of your sleepover, a list of who was there, what food you ate, and anything else you did.

Things to do

- Get together your favorite indoor games (cards or board games), so that you can sit on the bed or floor and play them.
- Keep a torch handy for telling ghost stories. These are best told with everyone huddling around the torch. For extra effect, cut a circle of paper the same size as the end of the torch. From this cut a ghost shape and then stick the circle of paper on the torch. When you put the torch on, a ghostly shadow will appear on the wall.
- Make a sign for your door to warn all adults to "Keep Out!"
- Put out plenty of bowls of snacks—popcorn, potato chips, nuts, and candies.
- Have a stack of magazines and comics handy (or get your friends to bring some) so that when you get tired you can snuggle down and look at them.

- Have ready an emergency video in case you run out of things to do and people start to get bored. This is unlikely, but you never know!
- Think up a forfeit for the first person to fall asleep—something funny but not unkind. You could perhaps put icecubes down her back, or say that she has to do everyone's hair in the morning, or wait on you all at breakfast.

Themes

Sleepovers with a theme can be even more fun. If you and your friends are into collecting Barbies, or Beanie Babies, or some other character, then make the party for them! Get everyone to bring their Barbies, or whatever, put up some posters, make up a few puzzles or a quiz about the characters, or have a swap session of spare toys or accessories.

Helpful Hints

Remember, your home is familiar to you but it may not be to your friends—and their parents. If you went to stay at a strange house overnight, you might be a bit worried, and certainly your parents would want to make sure that you were safe. So when you send your invitation, why not include

Sleepover Rules so your friends' parents can see you are being sensible about your party and your friends can feel easy about bringing something from home to help them feel comfortable in your house.

Sleepover Rules

Things to bring:
- pyjamas or shorts
- sleeping bag
- your own pillow
- your favorite soft toy
- a photo of someone in your family, or the whole family!
- snack food to share

Things not to do:
- jumping on the furniture
- throwing things at the light fittings
- going out of the house after dark
- teasing the family pets

Homesickness

However nice all the members of your family are—including your grandmother, your cat, your dog, and your gerbil—someone may still get homesick. Take this seriously. Tell an adult at once so that someone can take her home, or phone for someone to come and collect her.

Medicine

If you know one of your friends has to take any sort of medicine, get an adult from both families to discuss this.

Hands of a Friend

Long ago, in the 1400s, when families were larger than they are now and people were poorer, a goldsmith lived in a tiny village near Nuremberg. He lived with his wife and their eighteen (yes, eighteen!) children in an overcrowded house. The goldsmith worked long hours to support his family; money was short, and there was usually only just enough food on the table. But in one thing the family was rich—love.

Two of the goldsmith's sons had a dream. They were both artistic and they both longed to go to college and train to be painters. They knew their father could never afford to send even one of them, let alone both, so they made a pact. They would take it in turns to train. When they were old enough, one of them would go to work in the nearby mines for four years and use the money he earned to pay the college fees for the other one. Then the brother who had been to college would earn the fees for his brother to go, either by also working in the mines or by selling his paintings.

One Sunday morning, after church, Albrecht and Albert Dürer tossed a coin. It was Albrecht who won the toss. He would go to college while Albert worked in the mines.

Four years later, when Albrecht graduated from the Nuremberg Academy, he was already beginning to be famous for his artwork. His oil paintings, etchings and woodcuts were selling well so he would not need to work in the mine to earn money to support himself and pay for Albert to go to the Academy.

On the day he arrived home, Albrecht's family prepared a feast. They ate and drank and laughed and were happy. Albrecht turned to his brother, his dear friend who had worked so hard to give him his chance at what he wanted to do.

"Now it is your turn," he said.

Albert looked at him, tears streaming down his face. He held out his hands. "It is too late for me," he said. "Look at my hands."

His hands were ruined. The hard, dangerous work in the mine had smashed every bone in his fingers at least once. His right hand was so crippled with arthritis that he found it hard to hold large things like cups and hammers, let alone a paintbrush. He would never be an artist.

Soon many people were buying Albrecht Dürer's work. Today, hundreds of years later, his paintings and woodcuts are world famous and copies of them are still bought. One of his most well-known paintings he called "Hands," but it has been renamed "The Praying Hands." It portrays a pair of damaged hands, held together in prayer. They are the hands of Albert, whose friendship and love led him to sacrifice his own future for his brother.

Strange Friendships

Sometimes people look at two friends and wonder to themselves what it is that makes them like each other, because they seem so different. One may be sporty and outgoing while the other is bookish and shy; one may be very neat and tidy while the other leaves clothes in a heap and washes only when reminded, yet they form strong friendships that often last a lifetime.

So it is with animals; the strangest creatures make friends with each other. Here are a few examples.

Titan the Great Dane

Titan was huge and floppy and quite uncontrollable. He had been badly beaten as a puppy and had ended up in a pet rescue center, covered in sores from the beatings and very afraid of everything and everyone. His new owners, the Browns, had seen him there and taken a liking to him. They loved him very much but soon began to despair of being able to keep him. He was so nervous that even the slightest movement made him jump, and as he barked at everything that frightened him, he was barking most of the while. Sometimes he would also attack things he didn't like the look of, so much of the furniture in the house was soon wrecked and visitors had to be kept well away from him. Sadly, the Browns decided he would have to go back to the rescue center.

Then a stray kitten appeared in the

garden. It was winter and the tiny creature was shivering with cold. Thin and bedraggled, it looked desperately at Mrs. Brown, whose heart broke with pity. She fetched it a saucer of milk and then went back indoors to find a box to put it in so she could take it to the rescue center. She knew she had to keep it away from Titan. But as she opened the back door, Titan shot past her into the garden. She ran after him, terrified he would bite the kitten and kill it! Sure enough, he had the kitten in his mouth when she caught up with him, but he held it carefully and carried it into the house.

Mrs. Brown followed and watched in amazement as Titan gently placed the kitten on the hearthrug, then settled down himself and began to lick it. The kitten purred. Its eyes closed and it fell asleep between Titan's huge paws. From that day on, Titan was a different dog. He had a mission and something more frail and hurt than himself to care for. He and Ziggy, as the cat was named, became inseparable. Titan was mother and father to the small bundle of fur until it grew into a sleek, happy cat, when the two became friends. If Titan was spooked by anything, which happened less and less, Ziggy would either rub his head against Titan's to soothe him or walk over to the object, sniff it and look at Titan as if it say: "See, it's OK!"

For the rest of their lives they looked after each other. When Titan died at the age of thirteen, Ziggy curled up in a ball and died three days later. Life without his friend was not worth living.

Dilly and the Herring Gull

A bird sanctuary in Cornwall, England, rescued many birds over the years, healed their broken wings, cleaned oil from them and, mostly, returned them to the wild. Those that were too damaged to fend for themselves again either stayed at the sanctuary or were found loving homes. One herring gull had been attacked by a cat when he was a young bird. His wounds had healed but his mind had not. The shock had been so great that he shook all the while, twitched his head from side to side and was unable to stand. The owners of the sanctuary were wondering if it would be kinder to have him put to sleep when someone turned up with a duck!

Dilly duck had been a village pond duck. Happy to be the center of attention, she had lived there peacefully until one winter when the pond froze over and some boys threw stones at her, breaking both her wings. Dilly would never fly again. The people who rescued her kept her for two years but she was unhappy and they didn't know what to do for her. She refused to swim in the little pool they built for her and was now refusing to eat.

The sanctuary was short of space and they didn't know where to put Dilly. The only available space was with the nervous gull, but as he spent all his time huddled in a dark corner of his shelter, they decided to risk it and see what happened. What did happen was a miracle. The next day the seagull was standing, having been pushed into doing so by a quacking Dilly. He began to eat, again with Dilly shoving food at him and eating some herself to encourage him. He also swam because Dilly showed him how. Soon he was back to normal and was moved in with the other gulls. Then he collapsed again. Dilly, left on her own, went back to not eating and refusing to swim. Once the pair were put together again, the gull perked up and Dilly went back into bossy mode, eating and swimming happily. Together these two victims of vicious attacks survived, by helping each other heal.

Even Friends Argue

Yes, even best friends argue! The trick is to settle an argument fast and never to leave each other at the end of the day without sorting it out. If you each try and see each other's point of view, that will help. Sometimes arguments are over *opinions*, not *facts*, and there are as many opinions as there are people on the planet—so they're not worth getting too upset about.

If you can see the funny side of an argument and turn it into something to laugh over, that will help. Ask yourself what you value most: keeping your friend or winning the argument? If the friendship is more important, then swallow your pride and apologize, or make things up in some way.

One fun way to turn an argument into a game, is to settle it by playing **Scissors, Paper, and Stone**. This is a very old game for two players. The rules are:

Scissors win over **paper** because scissors cut paper.

Paper wins over **stone** because paper wraps stone.

Stone wins over **scissors** because stone blunts scissors.

1 Both players hide their hands behind their backs and make the shape for either scissors, paper, or stone.

2 On a count of "one, two, three," players bring their hands out and show which object they have made. If both show the same shape it is a tie.

3 It is usual to have three goes, the player with the highest score winning.

The Crow and the Puppy

In 1966 a South African newspaper told the story of an injured crow that had been rescued by a couple who had a puppy. The crow became great friends with the puppy and the two were always seen together. One day the puppy disappeared and could not be found, even after several days' searching. The couple then noticed that the crow was not eating its food. Instead it would gather some up in its mouth and fly off. Later it would come back, gather up some more and fly off again. After this had gone on for six days, the couple decided to follow the crow. They then found their puppy trapped in a snare. It had been kept alive by the crow, who had sacrificed its own food to save its friend.

Friendship is sharing an umbrella in the rain.